BONEGIRL

MANDY BROWN

'Bonegirl' is dedicated to my wonderful daughter Renate Brown. When it came to listening to and reading my stories, as a young girl, she was my constant number one fan.

As an adult, she has continually encouraged me and badgered me to put my stories into print.

Thank you for believing in me Renate.

CONTENTS

Chapter 1

"Give it back!" Rhea screamed at them.

The Scanlon hunters looked at each other and grinned. There was no way they were giving it back, not in a million years.

"Oh, this is so much fun! – our little prey Rhea the scared cat finally fights back," sneered Connie Evans, their leader.

Connie had grabbed Rhea on her way into the Girls' toilets and along with the rest of her gang; she pushed Rhea into the end cubicle. As Rhea attempted to struggle with her, she was pushed forward onto the wet, dirty floor; just as Connie seized her backpack. Terrorized, Rhea curled up into a tiny ball against the toilet as she covered her face with her hands and accepted her fate.

This was her life now; a regular part of it and not just some inconsequential part; and it made her nervous and angry at the same time. It wasn't fair, but no one cared. She'd suffered this torment nearly every day since starting High School. Through her fingers, she could see the contents of her backpack being emptied without any respect onto the floor. Kicks landed on her legs and shins, each one more painful than the last, but Rhea had already figured out a way of escaping the moment. She would simply tune off and pretend that this was happening to someone else. She was smart that way. Right now, she was watching a movie in which a poor girl was being beaten and although that girl looked like her, in this moment she was convinced that it was someone else. Yes, that was the only way to stay sane.

Connie's screeching voice jolted her back to reality. Damn! This was real. "No more to say? Pity!" Rhea glanced up briefly and in that moment, she saw one of the girls throwing her books into the rubbish bin. Unfortunately, Rhea's only retaliation was to slap the girl in her mind. She also proceeded to punch her in the face and…her thoughts were halted while she was still in mental motion. Connie's laughter was echoed by the others who made up the Scanlon hunters gang. Connie's taunting voice was the loudest; "Look she obviously doesn't want her things again!" On hearing these words, Rhea's tears came in quick succession as she sobbed out loud. What had she done to receive such treatment every day?

In the midst of her racking sobs, Rhea heard *it* fall onto the tiled floor and roll over towards her.

3

No way! The effect was enough to make her lift up her head. The Scanlon Hunters all stood, momentarily destabilized as they stared at *it*. The skull stared back. The seconds ticked by as each decided what to do next. The silence was broken by Connie Evans lifting her foot to stamp on Rhea's treasured possession. Why had she brought it to school? She should have known something like this would happen sooner or later; seeing as she was the choice scapegoat of the Scanlon Hunters.

"No!" Rhea heard her voice scream. Connie seemed to stumble, as her arms flapped like a baby bird and she flew backwards. Rhea reached out and in one desperate act of bravery, rescued the skull. The torrent of kicks from the Scanlon Hunters was inevitable – they had to blame someone for Connie falling and who else but Rhea their scapegoat?

Bonegirl – Rhea's Discovery

When they'd grown tired of their game and left, Rhea stayed curled up tight in the cubicle. She still clutched onto the skull. It was precious to her, despite what she knew would be the result of her holding onto it. The Scanlon hunters had added another name to their list for Rhea. She was clumsy Rhea, ugly Rhea, dumb Rhea and now weirdo Rhea. However, for the first time, Rhea didn't care. They could call her all they wanted but this skull was way too precious for her to let go off. She couldn't even stand them hitting it the way they hit her. It probably didn't make sense to them that she was clutching onto it so tightly since she'd never been able to defend herself with them before.

As she lay on the floor waiting for the end of break bell, Rhea recalled how she had found the

5

skull. One day, she'd taken the route home via

Shadow Woods and stopped to clean herself up.

That day Connie's gang had pushed her into a

muddy puddle and then spread rumours that she'd

had an accident in the toilet. The skull had been

sitting on a fallen oak trunk as if someone had just

left it there and in that moment, it called out to her.

She couldn't place her finger on it, but there

was something different about this skull. Rhea knew

she just had to touch it - the very symbol of death.

She was only twelve years old. The birds screeched

to her as if in warning as she picked up the skull,

but she knew she had to have it. Her hands shook as

she took the skull from its place and placed it

carefully in her backpack. Suddenly, she felt a huge

shadow as it touched her trousers. She quickly

looked behind her legs, expecting to see an animal

or something but she saw nothing. By now, Rhea was shivering despite the summer sun. There was something mysterious about this skull, and she knew it. Would she let go of it now, when she still had the chance to? No way! Rhea felt compelled to take it home, to have it live with her, for it to become her friend and feel every pulsing heartbeat of hers. It didn't make sense then and it still didn't make any sense now.

For over a week, Rhea kept it hidden in her dad's garden shed before daring to hold it again. As she held it once again after a week, she smiled - this skull was her own treasured possession; it sure felt like it. Knowing her mom, if she caught wind of it, she'd go mad. Her mom didn't even allow Fritz, their sheep dog, to chew bones! That was hilarious, but it showed the extent to which she despised anything that had to do with dead animals. As Rhea washed the skull in the utility sink she explained to her dog in a whispered voice,

"It's just a normal skull Fritz. Probably a sheep or deer's skull." Fritz sat obediently at her side. "This is the best one I've ever seen. It's brilliant. I'll show it to Mr. Mitchell in history."

That's why she'd got it in her backpack, but Mr. Mitchell, the history teacher never did get to see it (or maybe Rhea never planned to show him?) and the skull was just waiting for its chance to strike.

Chapter 2

"Silent reading time everyone," Mrs. Kay said, staring at two whispering boys. Rhea looked round. Adam winked at her. Connie was looking through her tattered photo album again. Rhea seen it briefly; in Mr. Mitchell's lesson on 'Our Family History'. Why did she always carry it about, anyway? Connie was probably too lazy to take it home or maybe her bedroom was so messy that if she put it down, she'd lose it; Rhea figured. That line of thought was appropriate enough to describe Connie, the dreaded leader of the Scanlon Hunters group. Sometimes the biggest bullies were the laziest people; why else did they like to make others feel so miserable? At least, that was what Rhea thought.

Katz flicked a piece of chewed rolled up paper at Rhea, but she just gave her a stern look. Rhea picked up her reading book and tried to read, but that wasn't about to happen because a buzzing noise was distracting her.

Rhea looked around, no one else seemed bothered. Adam looked towards her and mouthed, 'What?' She checked and saw that Mrs. Kay had her back turned before she mouthed back, 'That buzzing noise.' Adam shrugged his shoulders.

"Since when does reading require body movements, Adam Green?" Mrs. Kay's shrill voice echoed in the silence, having caught Adam shrugging his shoulders. It wasn't unusual for Mrs. Kay to pick on Adam, or anyone else for that matter, but her focusing on Adam made his shyness worse. The boy was barely able to speak up on a normal day but when under pressure? He simply cowered.

Adam fumbled and stuttered out something inaudible to her.

"Speak up child!"

Adam flushed up to the tips of his ears. Rhea spontaneously put up her arm, in an attempt to relieve her friend of this embarrassment. Mrs. Kay looked sharply at Rhea, "Get on with your reading! All of you!" she snapped. That was the end of the conversation, but the air of agitation was still very much present.

As Mrs. Kay got to her own desk, Rhea watched her sway a little. The teacher slumped down and buried her head on her desk. Several of them exchanged glances. Rhea was worried. Something was wrong with Mrs. Kay. At the start of the year she was great just like the other teachers,

but recently she was bad tempered and sad. No one

got that way without any reason, but Rhea couldn't

think of any reason for her teacher being so sad and

tired all the time. Could it be a problem in her

family? Rhea brought herself back to reality;

sometimes she wanted to help others so badly that

she forgot what she was ideally supposed to be

doing. "Focus Rhea, focus"; she chided herself.

Rhea, tried to go back to her reading, but the

image of the skull hiding in her backpack was

intruding on her thoughts. She reached out and laid

a protective hand on her backpack. Connie's eyes

darted in her direction. Just then, the bell rang for

lunch and Rhea instinctively, as if on cue, jumped

up and began running. She could hear Connie's

mocking laugh and, out of the corner of her eye, she

saw Connie gesture towards her backpack. Wasting

no time, Rhea ran out of the classroom knocking

Adam against the door in her hurry. She looked

back,

"Sorry, Adam." Adam recognized fear in

Rhea's eyes and his heart sank, as he knew that her

tormenters were on the prowl again. Rhea's

backpack disappeared round the corner as she

headed for the library just as Adam stepped into

Connie's path. She shoved him back, instantly

saying:

"Move it Spotty. Which way did weirdo

Rhea go?" In response to Connie's intense glare;

Adam shrugged,

"Towards the gym," he replied gruffly as he

rubbed his shoulder.

Finally, Rhea got to the dining hall. This was supposed to be a safe haven, she figured out so she stayed there for her food. No one was allowed to fight here and even Connie wouldn't dare. Rhea muttered a few words of prayer, hoping that today would be without any more drama. It was barely midday, and she was already tired! She did a quick survey with her eyes on the teachers. Mr. Mitchell's plate was full. Miss Jones had nearly finished. She sat next to Mr. Mitchell. It was always safer on a teacher's table.

As she began to eat her food, Connie appeared from nowhere and sat down opposite her. Her tray jolted Rhea's tray, but for once; Rhea's hand was faster. She held onto her drink triumphantly.

"Sorry," Connie said and glared at Mr. Mitchell's bent over head. She continued in that false sweet voice which teachers never seem to pick up on, "Can you pass me the water please, Rhea?" Silently Rhea handed the jug to Connie. "Please, Mr. Mitchell look this way!" Rhea pleaded in her mind as she glanced over at the teacher who seemed to be concentrating on his food. Slowly Connie splashed out her drink; and inevitably, water ran onto Rhea's tray. She smiled at Rhea, her eyes saying 'I'll get you soon.' All Rhea could do was avert the gaze as she tried to focus on her own food. Her life was officially hell; she couldn't escape from Connie and her group for even a few moments!

Mr. Mitchell broke the spell.

"Connie, how's your mother?"

Connie's face lost its composure; and Rhea noticed it immediately. Rhea saw a flicker of pain cross Connie's eyes. "Okay I suppose Sir," she replied meekly.

"Give her my regards," he paused "Connie if you want to talk anytime, just ask okay?" He stood up and walked off without expecting a reply. "Hmmm…something is going on there" Rhea thought to herself. What was there to know about Connie's mother?

Connie pushed her food around her plate.

"Stupid jerk," Connie whispered after him. Rhea thought she saw Connie's eyes water as she struggled to control her face. No retort, insult or threat was made as Rhea quickly left the table. Whatever was up with Connie's mother, it was very serious.

The home bell rang.

"Run rabbit, run rabbit, run, run, run," the Scanlon Hunters jeered at Rhea. The tiny stones pelted her backpack. One pinged off her head. If there was one thing Rhea could do these days, it was to out run the other girls of her year. Shadow Woods was her sanctuary and she only had to imagine herself being there already and in a couple of minutes, she would get there. Connie and her Scanlon Hunters all lived on the new housing estate opposite the maisonette flats. Luckily; it was in the opposite direction to Rhea's house, which lay nestled in Shadow Woods. They had never followed her into the woods yet and that was definitely good news for Rhea. Rhea looked back as she hitched her skirt over the stile. The Scanlon Hunters were nowhere to be seen. Her victory! Without further hesitation, Rhea ran into the cover of the welcoming trees. She hid behind a dense bush and listened. She heard a faint ruffle and then listened again; another ruffle.

Someone else was in the woods. Oh no! Had they followed her? Her heart was pounding, while her ears tingled with awareness. She could definitely hear breathing; someone else was indeed here. At first, she thought it must be the Scanlon Hunters or someone from school who had come to play a joke on her and the thought of that made her furious. Who were they to erode her sense of security? It was only here that she felt safe enough outside her house and if she had to fight to her last breath, she would do so if she found those wicked people here, behind her.

But now, after listening for a few moments, she was sure it was a man's breathing. Definitely not Scanlon Hunters and definitely not any other student. Her own breathing became faster as her thoughts ran even wilder. He was trying to move silently and carefully. Why would a man be tracking her? She could hear his watch ticking. What if he had been sent to kill her? What if he knew about the skull…or wait, what if he owned the skull! Rhea was trembling by now, as she considered at least 50 ways this story could end - all of which wasn't favourable to her.

Rhea chided herself. She hadn't done anything wrong really, and so no one had any cause to chase her so intently. She was being silly, he surely wasn't after her.

"Hello," she called out. The man stopped and she heard him change direction towards her. Instead of calling back though, he tried to disguise his movements even more. Rhea stood still. She'd lost him. A twig cracked to her right and she heard the man breathing again. His breathing rate seemed faster now. Rhea wanted to call out again, but a hare suddenly appeared next to her. If she reached out she would have been able to stroke it. Rhea was shocked but really pleased to be so close. His eyes held hers. She sensed that it wanted her to stay still. Rhea crouched down even lower, next to the hare. From here she couldn't see the path.

The man passed by their hiding place. He was holding a shotgun and a rabbit was draped over his shoulder. Her parents had told her many times to keep out of the woods in the hunting season, but this was June. Maybe he was a poacher. Rhea nodded a thank you to the hare, which disappeared almost immediately. She breathed deeply as she heaved a sigh of relief. The hunter had been after the hare, not her.

It was then that Rhea saw something glimmering under the ferns. As she peered closer, the ferns moved and shook slightly - then the glimmering thing was gone. In its place was an unusual bone. How weird was this? Rhea didn't think about the weirdness of it at all, she only thought about how fascinating it was and how she couldn't stop herself from taking it home.

Finally, Rhea picked it up,

"I'll put this with the skull," she said. She put it in the zip up pocket of her backpack. Next, her fingers began to vibrate strangely and she looked at her hands in amazement. She shook her head as if to gain more clarity on what was happening to her fingers. "Strange, where did all this green on my fingers come from?" As she looked at it the green tinge seemed to disappear into her skin. She shook her head again; "It must have been the light" she decided and walked towards home; automatically sniffing the air.

She was satisfied with today; at least she hadn't gotten beaten and there was a plus - she also had a new bone.

Chapter 3

Rhea's bedroom was tiny, and she loved to decorate her walls with posters which some people might consider weird but which she deeply resonated with. Rhea's room felt like home to her, and it was one of the places she felt safe and accepted. Her mom let her put up her posters, but had gone ballistic over the anti-cruelty to animal ones. They'd shown graphic photos of suffering animals in testing laboratories and neglected pets rescued by the RSPCA.

"You won't be able to sleep with these horror pictures. Take them down now!" she'd shouted, averting her own eyes. Rhea didn't get why her mom was so pissed. They were posters which reminded her of reality, and she felt every other person should also appreciate being reminded of what their choice of food meant to these animals.

"But mom, it's for visitors to realise what's happening out there, hidden away behind all the fluffy bunny pictures."

"No, Rhea; take them down. I know you love animals, but they'll give you nightmares." Her mom had said with a note of finality that Rhea knew better than to question. When her mom had gone, she gently took down the offending pictures and put them in her special box marked 'Cruelty to Animals Project'. Her hand touched the strange skull. She'd hidden it in that box because she knew that her mom would never open it and the skull was no longer safe in her backpack. She pulled it out and held it up in the light. The jaw of the skull seemed to lighten, then vibrate. A surge of static energy shot down it and into her hand. Rhea's eyes popped instantly.

"Ouch!" Rhea exclaimed as she instantly dropped the skull on to the bed. She glared at it. It looked dull and lifeless now, like a normal skull should. She shook her head, "I'm sure I didn't imagine that." There was something about this skull! Slowly Rhea stretched out her fingers and examined the outline of the skull. They seemed normal enough. As she continued her inspection and examination, the door opened behind her and her mom glanced at the walls, a nod of satisfaction following her glance.

"Rhea do you mind taking the dog for a quick walk, I need to type up some invoices before dinner?"

"Yeah, no problem," Rhea replied quickly and sat on the bed in time to hide the skull. "I'll just get changed first."

Right then, the strangest thing happened. When she stood up to retrieve it, the skull had gone. She searched under the bed, between the covers, the surrounding area, but her skull had well and truly disappeared. This was unusual, but before her mum would come again, Rhea decided to walk the dog. She'd better keep this strange skull thing private if she didn't want all hell to break loose…her mom had zero chill!

Fritz loved his walks. Being a sheep dog, he needed loads of exercise and he never seemed to tire of them. After a long walk of several miles; he would still be racing round, giving his ball to any willing person to throw for him. Indeed, he was delightful and wherever he went, people loved him. Rhea nuzzled him close to her face and then got a flash of inspiration. Their day was about to get so much more fun!

"Let's not go to the woods today Fritz. How do you fancy a walk through the fields and up to Callow Hill?" Fritz jumped up and down around Rhea's legs in excitement, snapping at the lead in her hands. "Come on. I'll race you." Together; they ran and ran till they reached Callow Hill. The climb up wasn't steep but Rhea took her time as she enjoyed looking at the emerging view. Fritz impatiently ran up the hill ahead of her, then back down again to encourage her along. At the top Rhea pointed out,

"There's our house and then the woods. Past the woods is Scanlon School and opposite that behind the flats you can just see the new housing estate. Connie Evans, the bully from hell, lives there Fritz." As she mentioned Connie's name, Rhea's face contorted into a frown. Fritz nuzzled her legs and licked her hand as she patted him. "Let's go back down."

As soon as they were in the field, Rhea rolled in the grass before she lay down; and proceeded to look up through the branches and leaves of her favourite tree. This was bliss. Her hands combed through the grass and daises. She felt peaceful again – school and home seemed so distant here. Her finger caught on something and she sat up to examine the object. It was a small hard lump covered in compacted soil. She scratched and knocked the soil away to reveal a tiny bone. As her

fingers touched it, the sun disappeared behind a

cloud, casting a shadow across the field.

"Where are you from, you little bone?" Rhea

inquired as she turned it over gently. Standing, she

pulled a large horse chestnut leaf off the tree. "Now

you stay on there while I see if I can find any of

your friends." Rhea started to dig by the roots of the

tree using her hands. Fritz joined in enthusiastically;

showering Rhea with soil, leaves, and twigs.

"Stop it Fritzy! Lie down." Obediently he

crouched down, wagging his tail. "So many little

bones Fritz. What do you think they're from?"

Rhea pulled some string from her pocket. Her

Granddad always said it was wise to always carry a

string, a tiny torch, and a Swiss army knife. Mom

wouldn't allow the knife yet though. She knotted

one end of the string as she began tying each bone to the string.

"Don't you think this is a magnificent necklace Fritzy?"

The bone necklace swung and clinked as she ran down the hill back home. It sang a melodious tune of its own making. In this moment, Rhea felt like a mighty warrior princess.

Her mother was by the door when she got home, watching her with horror-filled eyes from afar as Rhea approached the house. "Get that dirty, horrible thing off your neck!" mom shouted as soon as Rhea got within hearing distance. "You'll catch something." Uh mom was sure to object to Rhea's new necklace; with her insane desire for cleanness.

Rhea immediately responded, "No problem I'll wash and sterilise them all with dad's wine steriliser tablets." "Way to go Rhea!" She mentally congratulated herself for thinking of such a perfect response to her mom's objection. Mom stood open mouthed as Rhea reached for the bowl. Rhea herself was shocked; she'd never been able to think of a good reason before when mom would say 'give me a good reason for keeping so and so I'll think about it'. She liked this quick thinking necklace. It was the only thing she could think of that had given her such power.

Chapter 4

The next day at school, Adam and Rhea had gone to the library after school to work on their environmental projects, but it was closed. The notice said 'Staff Training'. The two of them stood in front of the library, mildly annoyed. Why couldn't they have their staff training someplace else, where no one would have to be inconvenienced? Now they had to think of someplace else to study.

Adam broke the silence. "You can come to my flat if you like. I have loads of nature books and I'm the only one who uses the Internet." Rhea was always moaning that her mom or dad hogged the Internet at home and she had to wait her turn to go online to do her homework.

Rhea's eyes widened at the suggestion. It was a good idea and they would finally get this environmental project off their backs. They walked together to Adam's home on the other side of town.

Adam led her up the stairs to his flat. It smelt of old ladies.

"My aunt's out till five. Do you want a drink Rhea?" Rhea nodded. Alone in the lounge, she peered at black and white photos. There were dolls dressed in knitted clothes sitting on the sideboard. A crooked faded print hung over the electric fire. The heavy net curtains looked rigid with dust. Then it happened. It attacked her from nowhere.

Rhea screamed and hysterically covered her head.

"What the ..?" Adam stood at the door scanning the room frantically. His aunt's budgie flew for sanctuary back into its cage. "Rhea what's wrong?" he asked, obviously scared, his eyes darting to and fro in search of what had caused Rhea to act so frantically. He put his arm round her – something he'd only fantasized about before. If it meant Rhea had to be scared before he could do so, he didn't mind right now. Adam smiled faintly. Rhea was such a sweet girl.

"It was horrible. It attacked me."

"You mean Joey? He's only a budgie. My aunt lets him fly free in the flat. He's harmless. Come here, Joey."

"No! Please, Adam shut the cage." Adam could not mistake the fear in her voice.

Adam liked her touch on his arm. His face flushed, "We can work in the kitchen if you'd prefer."

Rhea looked up at him. He had really penetrating eyes this close – they seem to stand out sharply as if the pupils were edged with an extra crisp outline. She made a mental note to go over why she thought Adam was cute. Or was he?

"Yes, please. I don't know why, but birds have always scared me."

Adam spread his books out on the kitchen table.

"I'll go and download that information about fox hunting for you and see what else I can find."

Rhea felt calmer now. "Sorry for being so stupid …about Joey."

"It's okay."

She liked Adam. Several times that afternoon she tried to sneak another look at his

35

fascinating eyes. He was more than a friend to her; a crush had begun to build slowly but unmistakably in her heart towards him. Adam Green!

She thought about his eyes all the way home. What made them so magical? She still hadn't figured it out.

As she arrived home, she could hear the clinking of her bone necklace. Her mom had let her keep the necklace at first, but had then insisted it be left outside. Rhea had happily hung it in the tree by their gate. It was like a guardian. She felt safer somehow, with it there. Walking under it she ran her fingers through it and decided to go for a picnic tomorrow in the woods with the dog. She might even ring Adam and invite him to come along. The idea fascinated her.

Bonegirl – Rhea's Discovery

Early Saturday morning promised good weather. She packed up her backpack with food, drinks and her art pad and headed off into Shadow Woods. Fritz bounded along behind her, his ball held expectantly in his mouth. He seemed to know that Rhea was up to something rather interesting. Rhea responded by automatically throwing the ball every time he placed it in her hand and smiling at Fritz. After thinking for a while, she decided to walk to the far side of the woods. The farmer had mentioned to her mother that badger sets had been spotted there. She found a small clearing and sat down. Her eyes scanned the area as she searched for hidden clues. On second thoughts, she had decided not to invite Adam Green to her special outing, but to meet him in the stile instead. Maybe next time, she'd invite him but right now, it was just her and her beloved Fritz.

Fritz curled up in the shade while Rhea lay down on the earth. It was so peaceful here. Slowly it dawned on her that the earth was really noisy – there was so much activity beneath where she lay. She could hear the earth being moved by the worms, the cracking, and creaking of the rabbit tunnels, the stampede of the insects through the grass. How was this happening? She felt comforted by these sounds, safe. She closed her eyes and drifted into sleep in her safe haven.

She awoke with a jump. Fritz was up and growling at some bushes. Rhea placed her hand on him, "Shh, Fritz. What can you smell there?" Eyes alert, Fritz sat down. Rhea couldn't see anything in the bushes, so she slowly made a parting in the leaves to look inside.

"Can't find anything. Whatever it was, you must have scared it away." Her eyes came in contact with something that was lying on top of a huge dock leaf. It was as if someone had placed it there, gently and purposefully; aiming it at Rhea. She picked up the shiny bone. It felt warm. Fritz rolled over, displaying his stomach in a pose of submission. Rhea laughed, "Okay Fritzy. I suppose you want a tummy rub now?" She rubbed him with one hand and placed the bone in the zip up compartment of her backpack. She glanced at her watch. It would soon be time to meet Adam at the stile.

Rhea walked cautiously back along the path. She felt she was missing something important and it called out at her to discover it. Fritz jumped over a fallen tree and barked excitedly. She leant over to find him springing up on all fours and pointing with his nose to a small pile of leaves.

"What have you found?" Fritz stilled his body and using his paw, he gently moved the leaves. Another bone. "Go on then, you can have it." Rhea said, dismissively. There was no harm in giving Fritz this bone, she would always have the opportunity to collect some more. But, Fritz sat down and simply looked at her. Didn't he want the bone? Rhea leant over the old tree trunk. Its moss left stains on her jacket while its twigs scratched her arms. She offered the bone to the dog again. Since when did Fritz ignore a free bone meal? He got up and walked straight passed her, jumped over the trunk and trotted off down the path. "Okay, strange dog turning down a free bone. I'll have it then and add it to my collection." The new bone joined the other one in her backpack. They walked together towards the stile and had to wait a while for Adam to arrive. He was already late by 15 minutes and Rhea had started to get upset.

Adam arrived at the stile breathless, "Hi, sorry I'm late."

"It's okay." They both stood with their hands in their pockets. A silence hung in the air. Luckily Fritz rescued them by pushing a stick into Adam's hand.

"Good boy," he responded with a smile on his face as he threw the stick into the field.

"Let's sit by the tree over there. I've got something to show you," said Rhea. Adam looked at her curiously.

"What is it, Rhea?"

"Hold on…I'll show you right away" she said as she opened her backpack to show him her bizarre collection.

Adam examined the shiny bone that Rhea had handed to him, and after his inspection, he said, "I think it is part of an animal's leg. Maybe the size of a dog?"

"This other one might be a badger because I found it in the clearing where badgers have been sighted. I think some people set traps in the woods to catch them."

"Do you have the skull with you?"

"No, it …well sort of disappeared. I was trying to hide it from mom, and when she left, the skull was nowhere to be found. It was really weird." She'd told Adam about the skull in school and he'd seemed interested as well.

"What animal do you think it was from?

"I don't know, but from your books; it could be a hare or a fox even?" Adam examined the bones carefully. Fritz lifted his ears in alert. Rhea saw a dark shadow stretch from behind Adam and over him to touch her. She instinctively pulled back and the shadow shot off towards the woods. Hmmmn…strange; she thought.

"It's getting chilly, "said Adam not looking up. "Must be some clouds rolling over," Rhea said nothing. She knew there were no clouds in the sky at all today but one thing she was sure of was that there were weird movements all around them.

Chapter 5

The moon shone so bright; it lit up Rhea's room as if it was daytime. Rhea leaned on the bedroom windowsill, mesmerised by the disc of the shadows. Below it, another moon shone and rippled in the pond. No one was here except her and the moons. Rhea held out her hands to cup the moon in them. As it lay in her palms, she heard a howl. A haunting, echoing howl that vibrated across the woodlands. The moon seemed to respond. The shadows of clouds floated apart to reveal an even brighter moon. The howl rose again to the moon and Rhea felt it pulsate through her body. She lay her hand on her chest. She felt her throat and neck. No way…could the mysterious howl be coming from her body? This wasn't real, it had to be imagined. How possible could it be?

Part of her could hear footsteps coming up the wooden stairs, and they turned towards her room.

Her mom shouted, "Rhea, supper time." Rhea's eyes darted from side to side. The howling was unstoppable. She grabbed the curtains and pulled them together. The moon blacked out. Her howling thankfully ceased. She could not think clearly however, and so she knew that things were about to get stranger. Rhea willed her body to respond to her command but she couldn't ignore the feeling of impending doom that was welling up within her. The door opened. "Rhea, are you okay?"

Rhea didn't trust herself to open her mouth. "Mmm," she nodded. Her mom waited. So, Rhea had to follow her. As both of them walked downstairs to the table, wafts of roast chicken reached her nostrils – and intense hunger took over.

"Rhea! Stop that!" All eyes were looking at her in amazement. She froze and quickly realized what she had been doing. The ripped chicken hung from her mouth, juice dribbling down her chin. One hand held her snatched food, while the other was imbedded in the rest of the family chicken. Were those fangs she had?

"S-s-orry," she whispered, quickly dropping the chicken and covering her mouth. She wished the ground would swallow her because she just couldn't process her actions.

Her mom's eyes were wide with disbelief. Or was it fear? Her dad looked as shocked as Rhea. His hand was on her mom's shoulder as he said, "Go and wash your hands, then go straight to your room. I'll speak to you later." She felt slightly relieved, the last thing she needed was to look into her mom's eyes right now. Staying away was better. Rhea was more disappointed in herself than she had ever been in her life.

Rhea stared at herself in the bathroom mirror. What had happened tonight? She kept looking and looking at herself in the hope that magically, she would understand what caused her to act so irrationally at dinner all to no avail. When no answers came, she dragged herself back into her bedroom. She instinctively went to her backpack and pulled out the bones. She lifted the lid off her special box to put them inside, beneath some papers. The skull looked back at her. Rhea was both surprised and intrigued. How did it get there? What was happening? It wasn't enough that she was acting all weird, the skull also had to choose tonight to reappear? She dropped the new bones, slammed the lid back on, nearly ripping the lid's corner off in her panic. She lifted the lid again. It was still there.

Could it be that her mom had found it and put it in the box? No, her mom would have freaked out. Maybe her dad found it and put it there? No, he had no reason to come into her room. Its presence only served to confuse her some more. "Thanks skull!" she said out loud.

Her dad's knuckles knocked on the door. He opened it, hovered a while, then strode into her room. Standing above her he said, "Your mom's rightly upset. What's got into you lately? Your mom said you've been arguing over some dirty bone necklace you made, then over your posters and now that display downstairs! It's all a little bit off and I thought we could have a little discussion? Hormones your mom said, but I think something else is going on. Do you want to tell me anything?"

Rhea knew she couldn't tell them. She didn't even know what to tell them. She looked down into her lap, with tears running down her cheeks as she shrugged. She loved her dad very much and she knew he loved her as well, but he'd never understand what was going on with her.

"Nothing," she said quietly.

Her dad decided to dig a little further to see if he could come up with what was wrong with Rhea.

"Have you been given something?" he asked. Rhea swallowed and felt her body tense slightly. She'd been given something, well she'd taken something but how could he know…? "I mean, you know, drugs?"

Rhea relaxed, he didn't know. "No." she responded simply.

"Well is it problems at school? With that new friend, Adam?"

"No, Adam's just a friend dad."

"If there's anything wrong would you tell us, please?"

She nodded, "I'm okay…just feel a bit odd that's all."

"Hormones then, I'll tell your mother." Her dad sighed in relief. His job was done. He'd tried his best, but really what Rhea wanted most at that moment was a hug. She almost screamed at him to give her a hug, stay with her a while more but…

She lay back on the bed. She wanted to open the curtains to let the moonlight in again but daren't. She remembered what had happened with the moon only a few minutes ago. A shiver passed down her spine and she dived under the covers.

Of the trio of her dad, mum and herself, Rhea was the most confused. Hopefully, things would sort themselves out, she thought. Little did she know that hell was coming to her? Things weren't about to get better, they were about to get worse!

Chapter 6

"If we walk through to woods to my house I can show you where I found the skull the first time. I still can't figure out how it got into my box." They ran across the school playing fields. Adam cursed himself for not being taller when Rhea managed to get over the fence effortlessly yet he had to struggle. The woodland path took them into the cool air. He would do anything to help Rhea, his best friend through the confusing feelings she was having. It only pained him that he couldn't do more to help.

"Ouch!" Rhea yelped. "I just hit my head on that branch." They looked up. Something was caught and dangling.

"What is it?" Adam stood on his tiptoes to see.

"It's a tiny bat, but she's wrapped up in, I think - it's some fishing line."

"Probably from the pool at the other side of the school."

"I can't break the line. Have you got a knife?"

"Here," Adam was routing in his bag, "use these scissors." Rhea cut the line and held the bat gently in her palm. Together they undid the tangled line. The released bat held on upside down to Rhea's finger as she lifted her up to check for any injury. She stroked her belly. It was so smooth and silky.

"You're so cute." The tiny bat allowed Rhea to transfer her to a higher branch. "Hope you'll be safe here, little one." Rhea felt fulfilled because she had helped the bat.

"That was amazing. I'd never seen a bat before."

"Nor me, but now I see why they say a bat is a mouse with wings. Come on, over here is where I found that skull."

They both searched and dug around by the fallen oak trunk and in the nearby rubble of stones, but couldn't find any more skulls or bones. Adam stood back,

"Do you think these stones are from one of those burial chambers?"

"I don't know, but mom took me once to an Iron Age fort on a hill just over from Callow Hill - on the other side of the woods. So maybe?" A bird suddenly fluttered up from the bushes startling them.

Adam checked his watch. "I'd better start running home. I didn't tell my aunt I'd be late." Rhea was glad he didn't ask her any more about the other bones. She didn't want to tell him about what happened at dinner the night before. He was her best friend but some things were better left unsaid.

Rhea had double art the next morning at school. Dad had already left for work by the time her alarm clock went off. The atmosphere at breakfast between her and her mom was still cautious and too quiet. Rhea tried to talk to her about the little bat, but her mom became agitated and said,

"No more animal talk, Rhea. That's enough!"

Rhea only remembered after leaving the house that they were all supposed to bring in a small, detailed object to do observational drawing practice. Not to worry she was smiling now because she'd found a beautiful feather on the way.

"I think it's an owl's," she told Adam.

"Trust you to bring in some soppy feather," Connie's voice reached like an arrow into Rhea's and Adam's conversation.

"It's a special one – given to her," Adam retorted.

Connie burst out laughing. She was so loud that everyone was now staring at the object of Connie's fun, Rhea. "Given to her? Ha! I heard if you're given a feather it means you are a coward – someone knows scared cat Rhea well!"

Kaz arrived in the classroom and caught the last few words, "Rhea's not a scared cat, she's a scared mouse!" Laughter echoed in Rhea's brain. She snatched up her feather and stormed off to the far corner desk. She didn't want to be the butt of their jokes, but she had no choice but to stay in the same room with these people. In any case, the far corner desk would enable her concentrate on the day's task.

Miss Stanley opened the door, "Good morning everyone. Come along dears sit down. Connie dear aren't you supposed to be in the group down the corridor?"

"Yes, Miss." As Connie left the room, Rhea cursed herself for glancing in her direction. As usual, Connie was waiting for her with a snarl. She could hear Connie, above all the shuffling chairs, making fun of her still by squeaking like a mouse as she went down in the corridor. She would do anything to be rid of Connie!

Miss Stanley's voice cut through the hurt, "Great, I see you have all remembered to bring something." Miss Stanley handed out sticks of charcoal and chalks. Soon they were all concentrating on their objects. At one point the room became so silent and intense that Rhea had to check that everyone was still there.

"Brilliant detail Rhea dear. You look like you've finished?"

"Yes, I think so."

"Good," she turned to face the room, "If you have finished please let me know; as I have collected a few extra items I'd like you to draw." Rhea put her feather to one side and turned over a new piece of paper. Miss Stanley's box was

producing a range of items – a king of hearts

playing card, a striped tie, an oily set of cogs,

"Rhea, I think *you* should draw this one." Miss

Stanley handed her a single antler. "I had this from

my brother who is a game keeper for a deer park in

Scotland. He gets loads of these each season."

Rhea held the antler in her hand. She stroked

the smooth covering. It felt light, not like the hard

bone she'd expected at all. She traced its curve with

her fingertips. A shadow passed behind her,

bringing with it a strong pungent odour. She

glanced round but seemed to be the only one to

sense it. She chose a charcoal stick and

immediately; strong, bold lines covered the page.

She felt compelled to draw the missing antler too.

Rhea was pleased with herself as she realised that

her attempts to draw in the deer face looked realistic. She was shading in the eyes, which stared back at her as deep, intoxicating pools when the end of lesson bell rang. It looked real enough, but she still hadn't finished. Rhea wanted to complete the drawing rather compulsively, it pulled at her.

She was still staring at the drawing when Miss Stanley fluttered her hand in the air, "Rhea, take it home dear and finish the picture for me."

"Thanks, Miss."

The teacher moved nearer and whispered, "You can keep the antler – it's yours. I have plenty at home."

It didn't bother Rhea that Miss Stanley wanted her to have the antler at all. She was very happy because indeed, this was a teacher Rhea could love!

Bonegirl – Rhea's Discovery

Chapter 7

Rhea slowly put on her PE shorts and top. She re-tied her laces several times, trying to delay as much as possible. The other girls chatted and laughed as they trotted out of the changing rooms. Connie would probably already be on the bars, swinging gracefully. Mrs. Brennon put up with Connie's blatant ignoring of the rules because she was her star gymnast. She even took her to the competitions in her own car these days. Everyone knew Connie was a brat, but she was the kind of brat whom no one could ignore or even control.

"Today we shall be practising for our Open Day. Mr. Todd has selected this year seven group to demonstrate what goes on in the gym to prospective pupils and their parents. Everyone has to take part, not only gym club members." Connie groaned in protest and rolled her eyes to the ceiling. Some of the gym club girls started talking. Rhea heard them moaning, "They'll spoil it…people will laugh…it's not fair." Miss Brannon looked straight at them almost apologetically,

"Afraid that's school rules. Better get started. Line up for the asymmetric bars." The gym club girls still continued to grumble and eye the new comers.

Rhea shuffled to the back and looked down at the floor. Although she was slim, she always felt so clumsy and stiff trying to do set gymnastics in front of others. Her mom said she was a natural dancer, but Rhea had never enjoyed gymnastics. Much too soon she found herself taking hold of the bars. Things were about to get tragic and Rhea knew it.

"Swing and lift yourself up Rhea," Miss Brennon encouraged, but her voice faded into the distance as sniggering from Connie's gang drowned it. Rhea felt her face flush, her hands sweat and she fell in a heap onto the mat. Connie's laugh was the loudest.

"That's enough. Rhea, try again," Miss Brennon sighed. Rhea shut her eyes. I hate Connie and her stupid friends. I hate all of them she thought. She opened her eyes again and the gym seemed darker. The others in the gym looked distant and fuzzy. "Again Rhea," she heard. This time the bars made tiny squeaking noises as she griped them. "Trust yourself," she heard. Rhea shut her eyes. She felt her body swing and lift onto the bars. The squeaking noises began to sing to her movements. She felt like she was dancing and shutting out everything, but the sonic like squeaks, as she went through the set movements she'd seen Connie do so many times before. She dismounted and landed softly on the mat. Rhea opened her eyes to stunned silence. One of the gym club girls started to clap, followed by everyone except Connie and her gang. Why were they clapping for her? Surely, there must have been a mistake. Miss Brannon stared at her,

"That was brilliant Rhea. Where have you been hiding? Which Club are you attending? It's a transformation – you were so graceful and powerful."

"I don't know," she replied truthfully.

Connie pushed forward to stand next to Miss Brannon, "Liar! She's just trying to show off. Miss Brannon, can I show you my new routine – I've been practising real hard?" Rhea shuffled to the end of the row. Several girls still stared at her. Rhea felt a new glow of pride in her cheeks. How had she done that? She honestly didn't know, but she would find out.

"Did you really swoop and glide like a bird?" Adam asked. He was beaming, "bet Connie was annoyed. You'd better watch out."

"I guess so, but it's strange I wasn't even bothered about being upside down or heights today. Yeah, and what were those noises? When the other girls went on the bars I heard nothing, no squeak, no creak or anything?"

Adam scratched his head, "I've been thinking about these strange things that keep happening around here. Do you think the school's haunted?"

"No, how'd you work that out?"

"Like when Connie fell over – maybe a ghost did something. Then there are the weird noises you keep hearing. Maybe a ghost of a bullied school kid?"

"Don't be silly! Since those things have been happening around where I am, could it be that there is something wrong with me?"

Adam laughed, "Yeah, maybe you're possessed by the ghost of the bullied teenager."

"I'm going to get you, whoooaa!" She stood up shaking her ghostly arms at him. "Come on break's nearly over."

During the next lesson, Holly Bishop started acting strangely. Mr. Mitchell had gathered the class round the front desks. Rhea was waiting her turn.

Six students had to present their environmental projects during this lesson. Rhea had worked hard on her research and she was fairly confident that she could make a good presentation. She felt into her backpack to check that the skull and bones were all still in there before patting them ever so lightly.

A girl knocked on the door and gave Mr. Mitchell a note.

"I'll be two minutes. I need to get something for Mrs. Finch urgently from our storeroom. The storeroom was only next-door. Rhea sensed her name being whispered. Holly moved over to stand next to Rhea. She looked flushed and Rhea could hear her breathing. Holly had been at junior school with Rhea. She was a very quiet girl and Rhea had often wondered why no one picked on her. Why did it always have to be her that was picked on? Rhea felt the deer antler at the side of her backpack.

Should she show Holly her bones now? Maybe they

could be friends, you know.

Holly started to giggle. Rhea turned to her.

Holly's eyes grew frighteningly larger and whiter.

Suddenly Rhea's vision blurred. She blinked several

times, which seemed to make the room spin. She

knew her eyes were now shut, but she could see

Holly on her right, the desk in front, another girl on

her left *and* she could see a group of girls behind

her. Connie and her gang were pointing to Rhea's

back and edging Holly to do something. Holly

moved behind Rhea and had her fist raised. Holly's

fist was aimed at Rhea's backpack. It was all

beginning to make sense. The Scanlon Gang were

going to use Holly against Rhea!

In slow motion, Rhea scanned the scene. Nobody was looking at Holly except Connie's gang, Mr. Mitchell was turning the door handle to come back in and Holly's fist was coming crashing down. Rhea could see the inhumane effort in Holly's face ready to break whatever lay hidden in Rhea's backpack. Rhea's arms and hands flung into the air as she turned. She used her full strength to trap Holly's arm and propel her backwards towards Connie behind her. The girls scattered as Holly fell back, hitting her head on the table. Crumpled on the floor, blood spurted out of her head wound.

Mr. Mitchell immediately rushed into the class, staring unbelievably at Rhea and wondering what could have gotten into her. Next, he began to help Holly sit up, his own handkerchief over the wound.

"Connie, go to the secretary and ask her to send our first aider. Rhea Jones, I saw it all. What is wrong with you? There was no need for your violent behaviour. Go to the Head's office at once!"

Now, Rhea couldn't explain that Connie's gang had been after her, or that Holly was about to hit her backpack and her act was one of self-defence, because of course, who would believe her? School seemed to be making no sense these days and Rhea felt defeated. Things seemed to always be against her.

Chapter 8

Rhea collapsed down by a tree and sobbed. I hate school. Me - the bully? Why hadn't anybody seen? How had she seen Holly's move before she even moved her arm? It was still very puzzling to Rhea.

Mom had taken the phone call from school and of course, she had felt disappointed by Rhea's actions. Rhea couldn't stand her mom's disappointed silence any longer and had run off to the woods. Mom had looked so hurt. No one believed her that Holly had attacked first. She felt sure Holly had been dared to break the fragile skull and anything else in Rhea's backpack so that she could join Connie's Scanlon Hunter gang. She could still hear Mr. Todd, the headteacher, shouting.

She could still smell his breath and anger as he spat out the words in disgust,

"This behaviour will not be tolerated at Scanlon School. We do not tolerate bullies! Any further complaints and you will be suspended."

Rhea looked up at the sky through the leaves. What was happening to her? She'd never seen mom so upset or been so confused herself. Tears trickled down Rhea's face.

She bit her bottom lip and spoke aloud,

"I didn't know I was that strong. I didn't mean to hurt Holly." Her sobbing slowly ceased and she began to feel calmer. The tree felt warm and strong behind her back. She felt its rough bark and had a sudden urge to climb it. Another fallen trunk lay on the ground next to it. She'd sat on that one when she'd first ran away sulking. She climbed on

73

that one before stretching up to the first oak branch. She swung her feet on to the oak's trunk and walked sideways up. Heaving herself up, she scrambled onto the first branch. Higher and higher she climbed. Her heart beat fast, and her scared breathing showed the strain of the climb. Her hands soon felt sore and her arms were beginning to get covered in scratches. Finally, she sat on a top branch and peered out through the leaves. This felt so magical.

She'd never been so high. A shuddering rush ran through her body – fear. How would she get down? She hated heights. Looking down to the ground; a new panic surged through her, but she slumped back into the safety of the trunk and branches. She had to think, to figure out what was going on in her life.

Bonegirl – Rhea's Discovery

Through the silence, she could hear the noises of the woodland. She listened. She heard the birds' songs grow in volume and variety till it was like an orchestra. She heard the creaking trees, swaying branches and rustling leaves in percussion. A voice floated on the music,

"Boon, boon, boon." She squeezed her eyes shut and shook her head. Still, the voice came, "Boon, bone, bone." She picked out the word bone and listened again, "Bone, bone, and bone girl." Bone girl? She opened her eyes. Two large round orange eyes of an owl blinked at her. Instantly Rhea felt herself zoom into the eyes. She blinked and saw a girl's face – her own face seen so often in the mirror - Rhea was in front of her and was staring blankly back.

Rhea's vision sharpened like when the optician puts in corrective lenses. Yet, she could see on both sides and behind herself too. Images of the woodland from high above the tree tops flashed by. She could hear the wind whistling past her ears as the air moved out of her way. She saw Scanlon School. There were some boys playing round by the sheds. She saw the pools with a few relaxed fishermen eating their packed sandwiches, Adam's flat glinting in the setting sun and Connie's estate with gangs of kids kicking footballs or just hanging around. Rhea blinked twice. There was an ambulance outside Connie's house. Someone was being carried into it, followed by Connie's mom. A woman was crouched down, talking to Connie. She wanted to see more but this journey was too fast to stop. She saw her own home. Her mom was standing in the garden shouting her name. She looked really worried and had been crying. Dad was striding towards the woods.

"Mom! Dad!" she shouted. The owl flapped her wings in front of Rhea's face. She opened her eyes and took a sharp intake of breath. Her fear of birds were rising to the surface.

Rhea was falling. She wanted to scream, but her tongue was stuck to the roof of her mouth and her throat was dry. "This is the end" Rhea thought. She heard the branches breaking and the tearing of her clothes. She saw the sky rushing away from her. Thud! Bits of leaf, dirt, and grass swirled in the air around her. Then blackness swarmed in and covered her.

She was still dazed but was sure no bones were broken. She grew aware that someone was

stroking her head and singing soothing words to her.
Rhea felt as if she was being cradled in big, strong
arms.

"Dad?" Rhea sat forward to see. The green
mist which had been surrounding her swiftly
cleared.

Her dad was running towards her,

"Rhea, are you okay?" His hair was ruffled
and his clothes muddy and torn too. "You're hurt.
What happened?" Confused, Rhea burst into tears.
Her dad rushed over and wrapped his arms round
her, "it's okay. It's all going to be okay." He
smoothed back her hair and kissed her gently on the
forehead. He sat on the ground and rocked her. She
felt comforted and in that instant, all seemed fine.

Rhea enjoyed her few days off school to
recover, but all too soon she was putting on her

uniform. She sighed; she knew she had to face them

sometime, and that sometime was today. It was sad,

but there was nothing she could do about it.

Resignedly, Rhea sighed and trudged on to school, a

place she would rather not be at.

Chapter 9

The toilets stank of filth and fear. She waited in her own trap for the hunters of Scanlon School. Rhea was too frightened to come out of the cubicle, but she'd been desperate today to go to the toilet and although she'd weighted her options, she didn't have any other choice. She was sure they were outside her door now. She'd have to wait for the bell. It meant being late for her maths lesson, so she was sure to get detention.

She sat on the loo and opened her backpack. On impulse this morning, she'd put one of the bones in there. She picked it up. It felt so comforting to hold. She'd try and get to the library at dinnertime to get that book on animal skeletons. She pictured herself being surrounded by the Scanlon Hunters. She tried to imagine being strong enough to stand up to Connie. She acted out in her mind what she'd say and how Connie would be scared and beg her,

"Please don't hurt me. I'm sorry." She imagined herself fighting back, but winning this time. She saw Connie and her gang lying on the floor crying like babies. She felt sick and angry. She saw herself hitting them, ripping their clothes, kicking and punching them. She could feel the savage reaction taking hold of her. Survival of the fittest – fight or flight. In this dream, she was fighting to live. Blood splattered over the walls, her nails long and jagged tore at them. Rhea fought like an animal defending herself from her prey and becoming the hunter. She would fight to finish, tear them up to pieces if she had to!

"No!" she shuddered. That's not right. She dropped the bone she was holding, but her own terrible thoughts upset her. It was horrible. She

could hear a humming noise. The bell was ringing.

Rhea felt frightened. This was a bad omen. She'd

get rid of the bones when she got home.

Fortunately, the Scanlon Hunters weren't waiting

for her at the door of the toilet and so Rhea heaved a

sigh of relief.

Adam offered to walk her home in case the

Scanlon Hunters tried to get her. He'd heard Connie

bragging, "Now that Mr. Todd and the teachers

think she's a bully, they won't mind if we teach her

a lesson."

Rhea avoided the path by the fallen trees

where she'd fallen and walked around the perimeter

instead. Adam stopped to tie his shoe lace again.

Rhea leant against the fence.

Adam ventured, "Rhea, I think there is a ghost at school affecting you, trying to protect you but it just went wrong last time."

"Maybe, but… " Should she ask Adam? He might think she was mad and then she'd have no friends. She opened up her backpack, "Do you think animals have ghosts too?"

"Never thought about it. I suppose so." He looked across at her and blushed.

"What?"

"I was thinking you're different from other girls." He jumped up, shoved his hands in his pockets and paced off ahead of her. Rhea smiled too, Adam liked her!

At the next stile, Rhea could see her house. She sat down on the stile. Adam had climbed over so he sat on the other side.

Rhea decided to trust him and tell him her thoughts, "I think the skull and bones have something to do with what's happening."

He didn't laugh. "No, my money's on the ghost theory. After all, if animal bones had ghosts, my flat would be bursting at the seams. Remember it was built on an abattoir." Rhea smiled.

"Thanks, Adam, you've really helped." She meant it. Adam had helped her realise that she couldn't throw the bones away. It was her overactive imagination at work and that was all. She smiled at him, "Thanks for walking me home. See you tomorrow then." Adam watched Rhea as she skipped through the field till she got to her house. He liked this girl a little too much; even her walking steps seemed so rhythmic!

Bonegirl – Rhea's Discovery

But other thoughts had engulfed Rhea's mind, she wasn't thinking of Adam as she walked home. Instead, as Rhea half-walked, half-ran home, she had a lot of disturbing thoughts. As soon as she got home, she ran up to her room and lay in bed. Her decision to keep the bones now meant she had a new problem. Where could she hide her bones? After the phone call about Holly, her mom and dad had 'a chat with her'; they had insisted she change her project – it was too violent; mom said. Her box had to go. Then there was the other problem. Rhea could not understand why the dog had suddenly taken to digging up her mom's garden – although she had her suspicions. That night Rhea decided to take the bones to Shadow Woods on Saturday and hide them by the old fallen tree. It seemed the best place as it had all started there. Drifting off to sleep;

her last thought was 'well at least School can't get any worse'. She had no idea that indeed it could, and it would.

Chapter 10

Rhea held her breath. Connie stood right in front of her. 'Don't turn round, don't turn round,' Rhea chanted silently in her head.

"When I find you I'm gonna crush you like an ant!" Connie turned round sharply and stared straight at Rhea.

'Please wall swallow me up,' Rhea muttered.

"Strange," said Connie, "I thought she was, someone was there?"

Rhea didn't know this cruel game. She opened her mouth to speak, but Kaz, one of Connie's, shouted,

"In here, I think she's hiding in the P.E. cupboard." Connie raced off after Kaz.

Alone again; Rhea broke her frozen pose. As she lifted up her hand she thought she could, for a few seconds, see the floor shimmering through it.

"Rhea Jones, why aren't you in your lessons?" Mr. Todd, the headmaster demanded. "If I see you skiving again this week, you'll be visiting my office." Rhea could never think of anything to say to him. She always felt so guilty even when she'd done nothing wrong, just like right now.

She scuttled into the art room and sat down in the only available seat, next to Adam. Connie's spies, Kaz and Gemma were already in the room. They grinned at each other. Gemma tapped her watch.

"As it's the last week of the term you can paint whatever you want; but please remember all the techniques and methods we've been working on," said Miss Stanley to the class. Miss Stanley had always been kind to Rhea. She once confided in her that she herself had been a victim of bullying when she'd been at school, but Rhea had said nothing in response, only feeling as if for once, someone could understand how it was to walk and run in her shoes.

Rhea felt a shaft of sunlight warm her arm. She could see the top of the trees from Shadow Woods while looking out the windows in this room. She relaxed. She loved art. Her paints flew across the page.

"A very unusual perspective; Rhea dear. Excellent observation work. Clever use of colours, but why all the different shades of red?"

Rhea shrugged. She didn't know why herself, "It just felt right, Miss."

"Good, good. Adam; great work!"

"Miss," Adam asked, "can I go to the toilet?"

"Yes, go on then, but be quick." As Adam disappeared out of the door, Miss Stanley moved on.

Rhea felt Kaz tracking towards her.

"Oops, sorry Rhe-ah." She knocked Rhea's arm. Gemma was shadowing her. She reached over and plucked Rhea's folder off the desk. Rhea looked around for help. No one cared to notice. As she made a grab for her folder Gemma opened it onto the floor.

"Kaz, why are you over there?" Miss Stanley called.

"Rhea dropped her folder, Miss. We're just helping her pick up her work." Hidden behind the table, Kaz and Gamma's hands scrunched up Rhea's work and creased it into the folder. Rhea felt her anger rising.

"Rhea dear, pass me your folder work." Miss Stanley put a hand on Rhea's shoulder. Pulling away in a snap, Rhea hissed at her.

"Rhea?" Miss Stanley snatched her hand back. Rhea sprang up from her chair, seized her backpack and backed to the door.

"Rhea dear what's wrong?" Miss Stanley took a step forward. She had to immediately duck as Rhea threw the nearest missiles to hand – the brushes followed by the glue pots and scissors into the room. Everyone dived for cover. Rhea ran. The walls seemed to move; the corridor closed in and became dark as if a huge shadow had formed over the school.

Panting, Rhea found herself by the girls' lockers. Her backpack was clutched tightly against her pulsating chest. Her fingers curled round it tense and white. What was happening to her? All she could remember was a strong overpowering smell, and then she'd hissed at Miss Stanley?

The one teacher who liked her was beginning to think she was strange. This wasn't good and as Rhea brainstormed to fix whatever mess she was in, she came up with no answers.

Rhea groaned; things had indeed, gotten worse!

Chapter 11

It was Saturday morning, and Rhea opened her eyes to the sunlight as it streamed blindingly into her room. As she slowly sat up, opening her eyes slowly, the overbearing guilt hit her in the stomach again. She sighed, instantly recalling that Mr. Todd had sent a letter home issuing her a final warning before suspension. Her parents had been furious. Apparently, one of the boys got a cut by his eye from the scissors she'd thrown into the room. What did Miss Stanley think of her now? Last night's talk with her parents made Rhea realise she had no answers for them, but she HAD TO find some for herself before she went mad.

She dragged herself downstairs. She could hear someone in the kitchen. Just as she passed the front door, the letter flap opened and a folded piece of paper floated to the floor. The note read:

> *Do not forsake the bones*
>
> *A friend*

Rhea was puzzled. What did forsake mean? She ran back upstairs to check her dictionary – it meant "abandon, give up on". Who had sent the note? Rhea needed to clear her head and think. Things were beginning to take an interesting note. She put the note in her jeans pocket.

Her dad hardly spoke to her that morning and mom still had red, strained eyes from crying. Rhea felt as if she had betrayed them all, and her insides twisted with a dull ache. She felt sick, lonely and afraid. The school letter was still on the table.

Bonegirl – Rhea's Discovery

Rhea walked slowly into Shadow Woods. Her bone collection, including the necklace, was in her backpack. She'd wanted to tear that letter into shreds - to make this all go away but even if she tore the letter, things would remain exactly the same at school. Raindrops started to fall. The clouds were heavy and grey above her. The drops were huge and loud. She quickly rescued her waterproof from her backpack. Raindrops mixed with her tears and dropped onto the back of her hands.

Rhea found shelter beneath some oak trees and impulsively closed her eyes to think and clear her head. The image of the skull set itself firmly in Rhea's mind. She tried to clear it and think of other things. The image returned again and again. She couldn't stop it. In her frustration she looked up into the rain, arms outstretched. "Go away!" she screamed, but the image of the skull would not wash away. Rhea wrenched open her backpack and grabbed this disturbing skull. She raised her arm in the air, ready to hurl the skull away when a movement in the undergrowth caught her attention. A hare stood upright looking at her, his head slightly to one side as if asking, "What are you doing?"

Rhea froze for a few seconds, then looked at the skull and back again at the hare's head. Was it a hare's skull? The hare's eyes locked with her own. She remembered that the hare had helped her before in the woods. She sensed that the hare was somehow connected to her. She placed the skull carefully down on the ground. As it wobbled, she momentarily took her eyes off the hare. When she looked back, he was gone, but she felt an excitement rising within her. She was on to something.

Rhea took out the rest of her bones and animal collection bits and placed them on the ground. She touched one of the small bones in the necklace. She looked towards the undergrowth. No animal appeared. Rhea closed her eyes. A flash of purple light behind her eyelids revealed the image of the bone she held in her hands. At the edge of her vision, a shape moved. It became clearer and clearer until she recognised it as a fox. The fox ran and camouflaged in with the trees. She knew it was there but could not see it. Or she could see through it, like the time she saw the floor through her own hand.

She opened her eyes and picked up the feather. Closing her eyes she felt as if her body lurched forward and she could hear the wind whistling past her ears. An oak tree appeared in her mind in minute detail and clarity. She opened her eyes and the clarity remained for a few seconds. With rising excitement, she surveyed the rest of her collection. Her heart rate increased and her hand shook. Her mind flew through the strange things that had happened to her recently.

She pulled her hand away. She was not ready to discover if any of these bones were responsible for that rage, fear, and anger she'd experienced in Miss Stanley's art class. Rhea sat looking at the bones in the hushed woodland. Are these bones really affecting me? Why? What does it mean? Can I stop them? A shiver ran down her spine and a feeling of dread overcame her. She sprang up, quickly dropped the bones into her backpack and started to run towards home with a mounting fear.

She felt as if the woodland was trying to hold her. Its branches barred her way, its undergrowth and roots made her trip and the boggy ground sucked at her feet. A "Bone, bone, bone," chant rose in her ears, getting louder and louder. Sweat ran down her back as she fought on. Not until she reached the stile, did she feel the woodland let her go. She looked back to see movements, strange faces, and dark spaces as if the woodland was alive with supernatural beings. She didn't look back again.

Lying on her bed, she tried to make sense of what had just happened. She had been scared but also stirring beneath her fears was something else. Excitement. A desire to explore, a willingness to get to the root of all of this. It pulled at her, more than she pulled at it but one thing was certain; this was not the end.

Chapter 12

The home bell had gone and most of the students had left school when Miss Kay came round the corner. Connie, Kaz, and Gemma had Rhea pinned against the corridor wall. Miss Kay pointed to Connie.

"Give me that photo album you're so fond of – now!" she shouted. Connie hesitated. "Now!" She fumbled in her bag and handed it over. Miss Kay opened it up and stabbed at a photo. "She wouldn't be pleased with your behaviour." She snatched over a few pages, "or them." She threw over each page. Her stabbing finger was creasing the photos making them distort. All the girls felt an uneasy panic as they swopped glances. Rhea saw a younger Connie's mother looking down on a younger smiling Connie dressed in a party dress and

101

hat. Then a toddler Connie sat smugly on a plastic horse on wheels, held upright by her dad. Spit flew from Miss Kay's mouth, her eyes white. She visibly shook like a taut spring ready to fire.

Miss Kay spat out, "Follow me. I'll teach you," and she pushed all four girls ahead of her down the corridor, out the door, across the playground to the PTA shed. She still held the photo album hostage as she pulled out the BBQ.

Connie remembered the last time her mother had to come to a school event – it was a summer's fete. They'd shared a beef burger. Her mom had laughed as tomato sauce had squirted out and just missed a passing teacher.

Miss Kay, with lightning speed, expertly arranged the coals, washed them with a liquid and produced a lighter.

All four voices screamed, "NO!" as the photo album was thrown to the flames. Connie reached into the flames to save it, but Miss Kay was quicker.

"Oh no, you don't, madam." She held Connie's arms firmly.

Sobs exploded from Connie, "But my photos." Miss Kay stood like stone guarding the BBQ. The plastic shrivelled, the photos disappeared as if through a time vortex till only the charred outer cover remained. Connie's struggling ceased. Tears and sobs filled the vacuum surrounding the scene.

Rhea could hear Connie's whimpering of despair and desolation. Yes, Connie was a bully but what Miss Kay did was surely wrong. Kaz stood with silent shocked eyes and a tear stained face, whilst Gemma wept openly. Rhea; confused and horrified let the tears flow freely and her silent sobbing echoed Connie's. Miss Kay simply walked away.

Connie dropped onto the grass, followed by Kaz and Gemma. Rhea couldn't bear the look on Connie's face. She looked so destroyed. Rhea hesitated then sat down too,

"Connie, I'm sorry," Rhea said.

"Those are the only photos I have of …" her voice trailed off into tears again.

Rhea remembered the vision she'd had of someone being taken to a hospital outside Connie's house. Rhea tried to think of a way to help,

"Maybe your relatives will have some similar pictures?"

"My mom looked so happy in those photos." Connie said sadly," She doesn't take photos any more, not since, well, since dad got ill."

Rhea had an idea, "Why don't *you* take some photos then? My mom's got one of those digital cameras. Maybe, you could borrow that and print out the photos at school? And, I'm sure we've got some photos of you and your parents from our junior school plays and fetes. You can have some copies of those."

Connie didn't answer. Gemma put her arm around Connie. A few pupils walked past the bizarre scene, but no-one asked and no-one interfered with the quartet of silently weeping girls. Rhea crept away to fetch Miss Stanley.

"Come on Connie love. Rhea told me what happened, I'm so sorry. Let's get you home to mom." Miss Stanley said when she arrived.

Together, all the girls walked away from the school

premises with Miss Stanley.

Chapter 13

Miss Kay was off sick the next day. Connie and the Scanlon Hunters seemed subdued, although, Rhea's sharp hearing picked up Gemma's stirring,

"It was all Rhea's fault. Miss Kay was punishing you because of her." Rhea, her heart pounding in renewed fear, had fled before they could do anything. She escaped into the classroom and stood by the teacher. Connie was bound to agree it was all her fault. Rhea knew there was no escape.

Year seven's field trip to Borth on the Welsh coastline was tomorrow. Rhea prayed that Connie and her gang would leave her alone with it being out of school. Her mind, however, supplied many different ways they could torture, humiliate and get her into trouble. She cried herself to sleep.

"Poor thing, she's covered in oil." Rhea glanced round for their reactions. She reached forward, but her panic responded to the seagull's self-defensive flapping.

"What's happening here then?" Connie pushed her way through the crowd. She stood so close to Rhea that Rhea could smell the ice cream Connie had just eaten. "Having problems?" she sneered.

"Don't hit her." Rhea couldn't bear the thought of Connie's cruelty aimed at a defenceless creature. Connie knelt down. Rhea would remember Connie's next action forever. She couldn't believe Connie would or could do such a thing.

Connie's hands had darted forward to pin down the bird's flaying wings. The bird was terrified and protested the only way it knew how – with its beak. Rhea focused on the trickle of blood running down Connie's wrist. Connie held the bird in a vice-like grip.

"Stop it!" Connie shouted at it. Rhea bit her lip, but her own fear of its sharp beak held her back.

Kaz started to laugh. "That's it, Conn – squeeze it to death."

"Shut up Kaz!" Connie shot back. Connie's one arm and hand held the bird tight, her other hand now held its beak shut. She was stroking its back with her fingers. "Don't just stand there Rhea – now what?" Connie asked her. Seconds ticked as Rhea's understanding shifted.

"Err, we could take it to the nature reserve down the beach. They'd know what to do." Connie nodded emphatically.

As the two started to walk in silence down the beach, Rhea studied Connie out of the corner of her eye.

Connie broke the stalemate, "Didn't know you were scared of birds."

"Yeah, but I'm working on it," Rhea replied in a whisper, "And I didn't know you liked birds."

The bird made a last attempt for release, but Connie re-adjusted her grip. Stroking its head she spoke to it, "Huh, I suppose we'll have a few scars to show for you after this is all over, but they'll heal. Hope you'll be alright."

Rhea blurted out, "Connie, I'm glad you were there."

Connie turned and at that moment Rhea knew there'd be no more bullying. "Rhea, thanks for saying those things about my photos. All that made me think. Miss Kay sort of showed me how it feels to be, you know, bullied. I'm sorry," she said. "Here, try stroking him on his back – I think he's beginning to like it."

Rhea felt warm as she stroked the bird and walked beside the girl who had bullied her all year. It all felt surreal!

On the coach back, Rhea sat next to Adam. She whispered,

"Honestly I stroked the bird and didn't feel at all scared."

"So Joey can come out of his cage when you visit again?"

"Maybe." Rhea turned away and looked out the window, "Adam, I think I need to go back to the woodlands. I know what I said about last time, but I need to know."

"I'll come with you."

"No, I need to do this alone." Rhea said with a note of finality, as she patted Adam's hand as if to say, "It's all right".

Chapter 14

Rhea strode into Shadow Woods. She was relieved but disappointed that it all seemed so normal. She sat down by the oak trunk and waited. Nothing was happening, so she started to take out her bone collection. A glimmer shape, similar to the one she'd seen before under the ferns, caught her attention. She held her breath. She calmly stared at it as it grew and took form. A semi-transparent figure of a man appeared – the green shimmer around his body swirling like mist. The features of animals momentarily formed in his clothes then disappeared.

"Hello, bone girl, Keeper of the Bones and spirits of the animal kingdom. I need your help. You can refuse as it involves the greatest of danger and possibly your life. You are the Bone Keeper.

Release the spirits of wild boar, bear, and dragon because I have need of them. Do so by the next full moon."

"Sorry? What? How?" Rhea's words stumbled out in panic.

"Has not your tribe passed on the ways of magic to you? Grave danger." His shape dimmed, "Ah, I see you hold the power of the fox. A wise choice. We have not had a Bone Keeper for many kingships. Can you remember how to release the power of the dragon for your people?"

Rhea opened her mouth but she did not know what to say. She shrugged at him apologetically.

"What do you know?" Rhea didn't respond. "You knew that the skull was the awakener of your senses and destiny's choice didn't you?"

"Yes," she replied quickly; trying to piece everything together like a jigsaw, "Yes, I remember the surge of energy, its glow, and vibration."

He seemed pleased with her answer. "Good. Do you know that the one who gave you birth is of the Bone Tribe? She felt the call but was too afraid. She recognised the signs of transition in you. We are pleased she wishes you to make your choice."

"Who? How do you know?" Images of her mom over-reacting when the dog brought in a bone, her mom's face when Rhea wore the necklace and the look in her eyes when Rhea grabbed the chicken flashed into her mind. It was all beginning to make sense, yet still seemed too impossible to believe. Mom was of the Bone Tribe?

"You carry her word in your pocket and her blessing to do what she could not." Rhea felt the crumpled note still in her jean pocket. The note was from her mom! "The skull will always find the chosen one and like its guardian, the hare, it too can remain still and unseen in danger. As the Bone Keeper, this skill is yours to command. But you need to learn to control the spirits of the bones. No more badger aggressiveness at your building of learning or wolf feasting at home. "

"But, I don't know how to control them."

"Call to their shadow spirits at first, then if you need to, you can direct their power through their bone, a feather or hair. With practice, you will be able to summon their help with the aid of just your mind – like you did with the bat in the room and with the bars that you swung round."

"In the P.E. lesson! Of course, the squeaky noises and what happened to me on the bars!" Rhea smiled. Her eyes revealed her happiness. It was all clear now. The fox helped her be invisible to Connie, the owl helped her see other people's perspectives more clearly and the deer's vision helped her see Holly before locking arms with her. A thought occurred to her, "The necklace?"

"As I said; you hold the power of the fox, with its cunning, quick thinking, diplomacy and invisibility." He fell silent – she had enough to make the choice. Rhea's mind was filled with racing thoughts. With a sudden urgency in his voice, he interrupted, "Bone Keeper, are you prepared risk your life to help us?"

Rhea nodded, a sign of her acceptance of the herculean task ahead of her. She didn't know what it would involve, but if this was her destiny, she might as well fulfil it. If not because of the man standing

117

before her who seemed to believe in her so much, she would do so in gratitude to the animals that had helped her these past weeks as she sorted out issues that troubled her at school. Filled with resolve, Rhea nodded again, and again, until the semi-transparent figure of the man glowed brightly, transmitting to her that he was happy with her choice.

"Bone Keeper, we will be with you to render whatever help we can. Thank you for choosing to use your powers!"

And with that, he disappeared and Rhea was left with the task of figuring out how to release the spirits of the wild boar, bear, and dragon. She didn't know how just yet, but with the fox and owl and deer still with her to aid her, she would embark on the adventure of a lifetime.

Rhea patted her backpack. This was her destiny!

'Rhea's Destiny MY BLOOD'

Book 2 in the 'Bonegirl' series:

"My blood……bone," Adam gasped as Rhea held his battered and broken body in her arms. He wasn't making sense. Tears ran down her face. She jolted and fell forward over him as something sharp skimmed her shoulder. "Collect … my blood before it's too late!" he shuddered out the words. His head sank to one side and his eyes stared open and lifeless.

"No, no. This mustn't happen. Adam!" A green liquid was oozing towards the two shattered bodies. Voices were shouting at them to move…

Please leave your review on Amazon about

'Bonegirl' so that I know you enjoyed it and are,

hopefully, looking forward to Book 2 in the

'Bonegirl' series called

'Rhea's Destiny MY BLOOD'.

Subscribe on Mandy Brown's website

https://www.nipplestokneecaps.com

for updates re new books, blogs and exclusive

information only revealed to subscribers.